Old MacDonald
Had a Farm

WITH PICTURES BY

Holly Berry

NORTH-SOUTH BOOKS / NEW YORK

Old MacDonald had a farm,

EIEIO!

And on that farm
he had a
PIG

E I E I O !

With an oink oink here
and an oink oink there.
Here an oink,
there an oink,
everywhere an oink oink.
Old MacDonald
had a farm,
E I E I O !

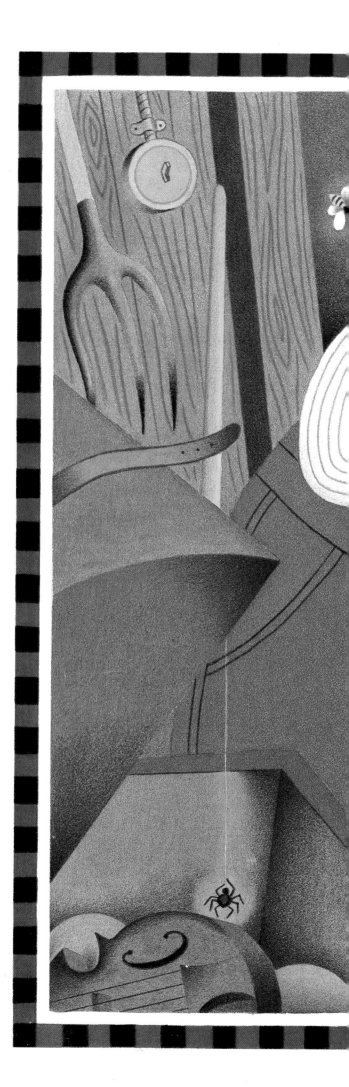

And on that farm
he had a
CAT

E₁E₁O!

With a meow meow here
and a meow meow there.
Here a meow,
there a meow,
everywhere a meow meow.
Old MacDonald
had a farm,
E₁E₁O!

And on that farm
he had a
COW

EIEIO!

With a moo moo here
and a moo moo there.
Here a moo,
there a moo,
everywhere a moo moo.
Old MacDonald
had a farm,
EIEIO!

And on that farm
he had a
CHICK

E₁E₁O!

With a cluck cluck here
and a cluck cluck there.
Here a cluck,
there a cluck,
everywhere a cluck cluck.
Old MacDonald
had a farm,

E₁E₁O!

And on that farm
he had a
DONKEY

E I E I O!

With a hee haw here
and a hee haw there.
Here a hee,
there a haw,
everywhere a hee haw.
Old MacDonald
had a farm,

E I E I O!

And on that farm
he had a
DUCK

E_IE_IO!

With a quack quack here
and a quack quack there.
Here a quack,
there a quack,
everywhere a quack quack.
Old MacDonald
had a farm,

E_IE_IO!

And on that farm
he had a
DOG

EIEIO!

With a bow wow here
and a bow wow there.
Here a bow,
there a wow,
everywhere a bow wow.
Old MacDonald
had a farm,
EIEIO!

And on that farm
he had a
SHEEP

E₁E₁O!

With a baa baa here
and a baa baa there.
Here a baa,
there a baa,
everywhere a baa baa.
Old MacDonald
had a farm,
E₁E₁O!

Old MacDonald had a farm,

E I E I O !

A Note About the Song

"Old MacDonald's Farm" describes perhaps the most famous of all American farms. School children long have learned how to oink, meow, moo, and make all the other barnyard noises from this popular nursery song. But Old MacDonald's Farm was not always Old MacDonald's and it was not even American. The earliest variant goes back to the early 1700s, to Thomas D'Urfey's ditty about English country life "In the Fields in Frost and Snow," in which the original refrain ran:

Here a Boo, there a boo, everywhere a Boo...
Here a Whoo, there a Whoo, everywhere a Whoo...
Here a Bae, there a Bae, everywhere a Bae...

Then new stanzas were added for other country sounds such as:

Here a Cou, there a Cou, everywhere a Cou...
Here a Goble, there a Goble, everywhere a Goble...
Here a Cackle, there a Cackle, everywhere a Cackle...
Here a Quack, there a Quack, everywhere a Quack...
Here a Grunt, there a Grunt, everywhere a Grunt...

Another version was popularized in the United States by Christy's Minstrels and other traveling shows during the mid-nineteenth century. This one began:

My grandfather had some very fine dogs,
In the merry green fields of Olden...

And the old plantation tune went on to introduce all the other animals grandfather had in his merry green fields.

During World War I the song—largely as we know it today—was popular with American and British troops but with one important difference. At that time it was Old *MacDaugal* who had a farm in *Ohi-i-o!* By the 1920s it was finally known as Old MacDonald's Farm, but this version had something still found in some barns today. On that farm he had a *Ford:*

Here a rattle, there a rattle, everywhere a rattle...!

With love and gratitude
to my Great Aunt Gladys

Illustrations copyright © 1994 by Holly Berry

Published in the United States by North-South Books Inc., New York.

Published simultaneously in Great Britain, Canada,
Australia, and New Zealand in 1994 by North-South Books,
an imprint of Nord-Süd Verlag AG, Gossau Zürich, Switzerland.

Library of Congress Cataloging-in-Publication Data is available.
A CIP catalogue record for this book is available from The British Library
ISBN 1-55858-281-9 (trade binding)
ISBN 1-55858-282-7 (library binding)

The art for this book was
prepared with colored pencils and watercolor
Musical arrangement by Perry Iannone
Typography by Marc Cheshire
1 3 5 7 9 10 8 6 4 2
Printed in Belgium